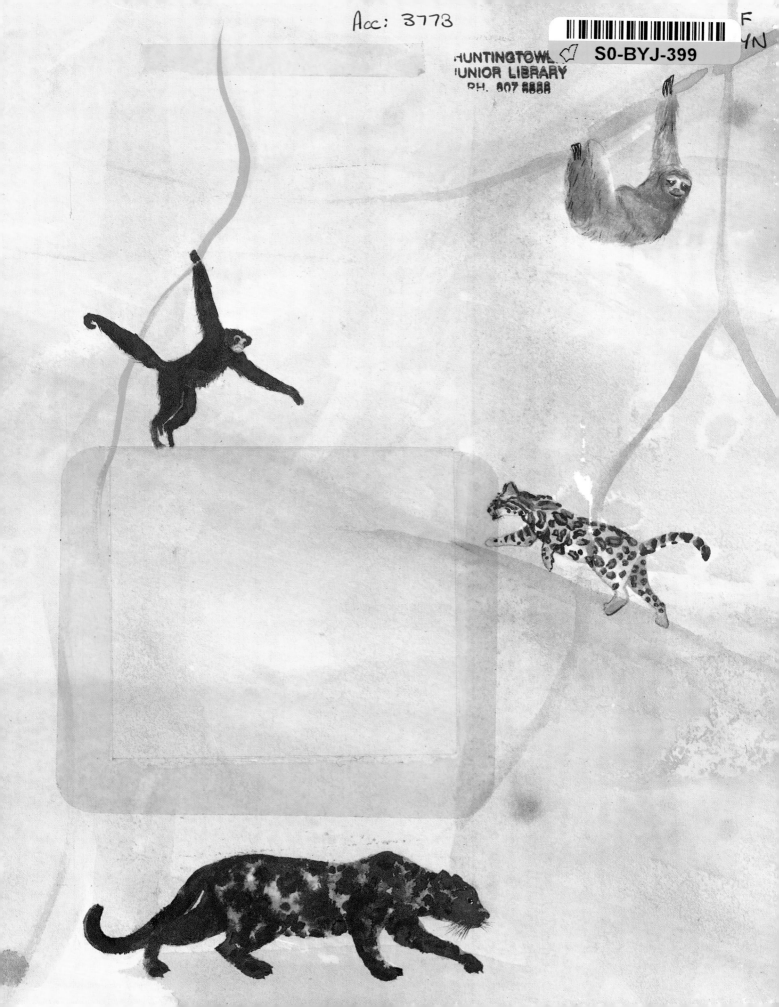

Collins

An Imprint of HarperCollins*Publishers*

First published in Great Britain by HarperCollins Publishers Ltd in 1994
10 9 8 7 6 5 4 3 2 1 Text and illustrations copyright © Tim Vyner 1994
A CIP catalogue record for this title is available from the British Library.
ISBN 0 00 198045 9 The author asserts the moral right to be identified as the author of the work.
Printed and bound in China. This book is set in Stemple Garamond.

THE TREE
IN THE FOREST

Tim Vyner

This is the tree
that grew in the heart of the forest.

On a leaf is the frog,
who sang in the tree
that grew in the heart of the forest.

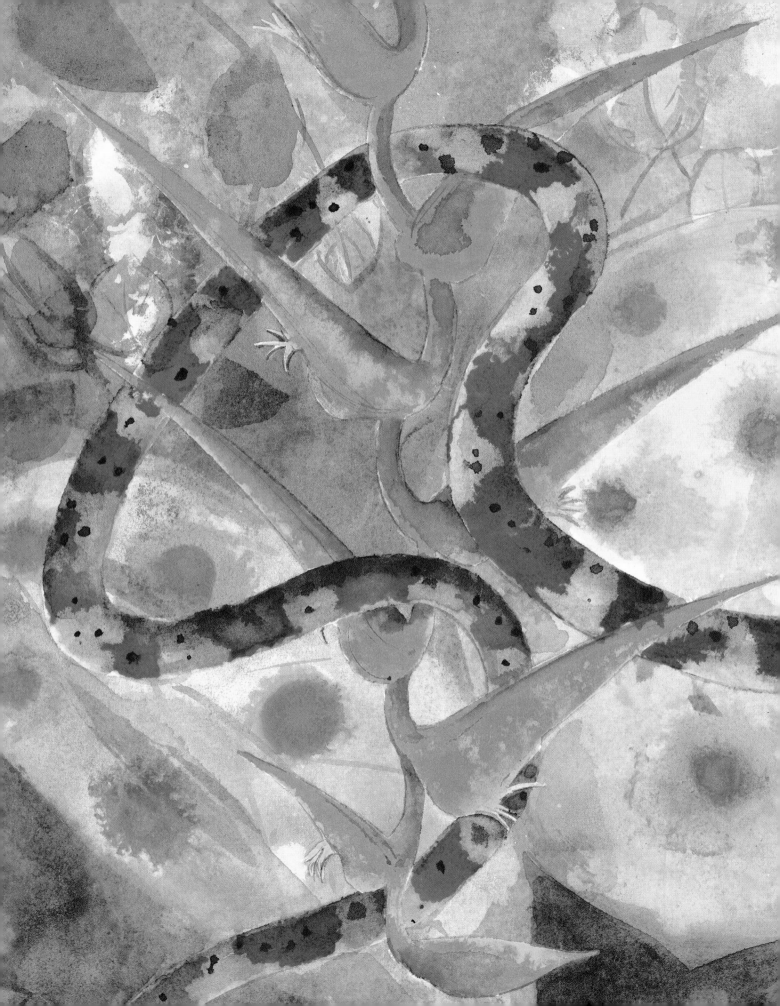

This is the snake,
that searched for the frog,
who sang in the tree
that grew in the heart of the forest.

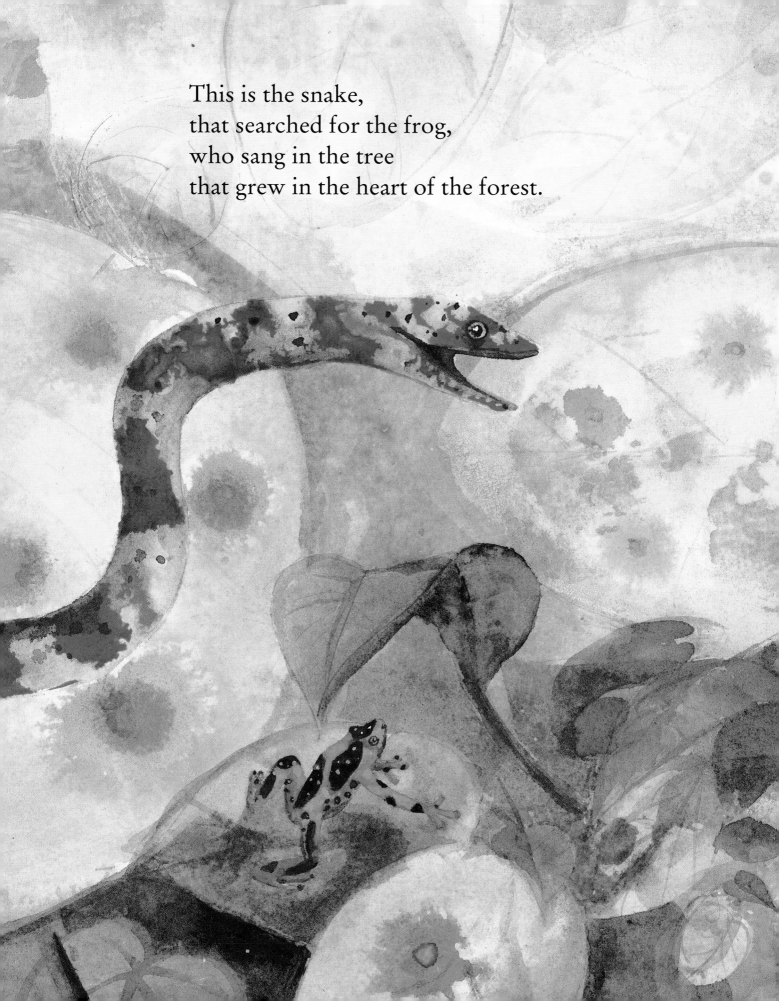

On a branch swings the monkey,
who missed the snake,
that searched for the frog,
who sang in the tree
that grew in the heart of the forest.

Here is the cat that leaps and pounces,
that chased the monkey who swung from a branch,
who missed the snake,
that searched for the frog,
who sang in the tree
that grew in the heart of the forest.

The three-toed sloth hangs silent and still,
who fooled the cat that leapt and pounced,
that chased the monkey who swung from a branch,
who missed the snake,
that searched for the frog,
who sang in the tree
that grew in the heart of the forest.

The racing tamarins who run with great skill,
jumped past the sloth hanging silent and still,
who fooled the cat that leapt and pounced,
that chased the monkey who swung from a branch,
who missed the snake,
that searched for the frog,
who sang in the tree
that grew in the heart of the forest.

The hungry panther, stalking a kill,
prowled under the tamarins who run with great skill,
that jumped past the sloth hanging silent and still,
who fooled the cat that leapt and pounced,
that chased the monkey who swung from a branch,
who missed the snake,
that searched for the frog,
who sang in the tree
that grew in the heart of the forest.

In the canopy a toucan, colourful and bright,
spotted the panther stalking a kill,
who prowled under the tamarins who run with great skill,
that jumped past the sloth hanging silent and still,
who fooled the cat that leapt and pounced,
that chased the monkey who swung from a branch,
who missed the snake,
that searched for the frog,
who sang in the tree
that grew in the heart of the forest.

The jewel-like beetle frozen with fright,
escaped from the toucan, colourful and bright,
that spotted the panther stalking a kill,
who prowled under the tamarins who run with great skill,
that jumped past the sloth hanging silent and still,
who fooled the cat who leapt and pounced,
that chased the monkey who swung from a branch,
who missed the snake,
that searched for the frog,
who sang in the tree
that grew in the heart of the forest.

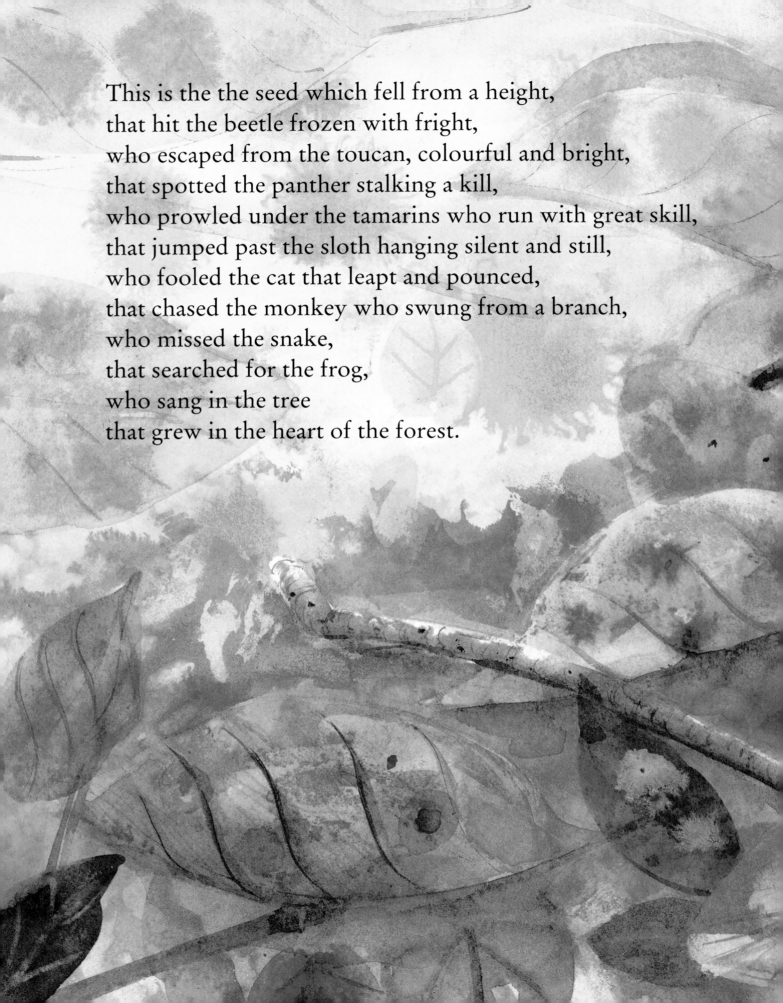

This is the the seed which fell from a height,
that hit the beetle frozen with fright,
who escaped from the toucan, colourful and bright,
that spotted the panther stalking a kill,
who prowled under the tamarins who run with great skill,
that jumped past the sloth hanging silent and still,
who fooled the cat that leapt and pounced,
that chased the monkey who swung from a branch,
who missed the snake,
that searched for the frog,
who sang in the tree
that grew in the heart of the forest.

This is the sapling standing upright,
that grew from the seed which fell from a height,
that hit the beetle frozen with fright,
who escaped from the toucan, colourful and bright,
that spotted the panther stalking a kill,
who prowled under the tamarins who run with great skill,
that jumped past the sloth hanging silent and still,
who fooled the cat that leapt and pounced,
that chased the monkey who swung from a branch,
who missed the snake,
that searched for the frog,
who sang in the tree
that grew in the heart of the forest.

TOUCAN

The toucan's brightly coloured bill needs to be very light because of its size. It is made of honeycomb shaped bone which makes it very strong. This helps the toucan crush hard fruits and unsuspecting insects.

BEETLE

There are more than 250,000 known species of beetle. They come in all shapes and sizes and they provide a rich source of food for many of the other animals in the forest. Beetles avoid being caught by camouflage or by tasting awful. Some have markings which confuse hunters. New species of insects are still being discovered.

TAMARINS

Emperor Tamarins get their name from their whiskers which look like an old Chinese emperor's moustache. Tamarins are small and light, which means they are fast and agile in the branches. Their tail is longer than the whole length of their body.

FROG

Some tree-frogs are very poisonous. Amazonian Indians use this poison to make arrows to hunt with, which is why these frogs are sometimes called Poison Dart Frogs. Their bright colours are a warning to other animals that they wouldn't taste very nice! They are very small frogs, just 1-5 cm long.

SNAKE

Vine snakes have very thin bodies which can reach out a long way from a branch or a leaf. This allows them to surprise frogs and lizards. They can measure over a metre in length but their body is not much thicker than a pen.